T0368305

On Christianity, Family and Fiction

A Book of Poems, Poetic Short Stories, and Other Short Stories

Amanda Libbers

AuthorHouse™
1663 Liberty Drive
Bloomington, IN 47403
www.authorhouse.com
Phone: 1 (800) 839-8640

Published by AuthorHouse 11/13/2018

ISBN: 978-1-5462-6840-6 (sc)
ISBN: 978-1-5462-6841-3 (e)

Library of Congress Control Number: 2018913606

Print information available on the last page.

This book is printed on acid-free paper.

authorHOUSE®

Dedicated to Mary Lou James at the Oh Baby! store in Baton Rouge, Louisiana, to Elizabeth Libbers, and to David Libbers and in honor and loving memory of Robert "Bob" Libbers.

May the legacy of Robert Libbers's expression of repentance for his sins, and of sorrow for those he hurt, live on!

Contents

My Father Loves Me More Than I Will Ever Know

My Father loves me more than I'll ever know.
He tells me through his words that I am the apple of his eye,
That he engraved my name on the palm of his hand.

When I despair, he reminds me of his profound compassion and love.
And in my Father is the One I truly love,
The One who is in my Father,
My bright morning star.
His love for mankind was the greatest,
For he traded his life so that we might be with him.

New creatures in joy we will be made
As sin and darkness fade away,
Forever in his presence all around.
His presence is in the light.

And when we finally meet the One who gave it all,
The One who made us his adopted children,
We will know true love and comfort
That we could never find in our lifetimes.

The description of the One I love cannot be put into words,
For he is always in the present—there for us simultaneously in time and eternity.

But in the love of my Father,
The connection I feel to my Father in heaven, is yet another one in addition to Jesus Christ.
He is part of the Father's Spirit. He is called the Holy Spirit.
The Holy Spirit is my helper, my counselor, the one who brings me

Unexplained peace and grace, the one who heals all sicknesses and diseases.
He is called the breath of life.

So what is the name of the One I love?
His name is the Father, and in him are the Son—Jesus Christ—and the Holy Spirit.
They are three in one,
All the same God.
They are one.
This is who my Father is in a complete sense, one God.
The Father, Yahweh; the Son, Jesus Christ, and the Holy Spirit. He is the Father whom I love.
The breath of life, the Holy Spirit, helps me enter eternity through Jesus Christ
When life's journey is over, a journey I began in receiving salvation by faith
And by asking Jesus to be my personal Savior and Lord of my life.

As I set myself on my bright morning star ahead,
Onward to heaven to God's presence I go!
My helper, who is called the Holy Spirit, is with me and in me always,
Carrying me home to my bright morning star—the entrance into eternity.
Seeing my bright morning star is like seeing the Father and the Son simultaneously,
For the Son is in the Father, and the Son is begotten of the Father, not made,
And is one in being with the Father.
And my helper, the breath of life, also the one whom I love,
Helps me travel to him, my bright morning star.
He is also part of the Father—the one whom I love.

So I journey home. My joy will arrive when I am there,
When I am made new and whole again.

But before any change occurred,
My mind began to wander.
I thought back on my Father's love in life.
How could I best describe his love interwoven in the journey?

Aha! I thought, *That is it—an analogy with learning to ride a bicycle.*
I think it will fit, though not perfectly.

My life on earth began one day.
On a beautiful sunny morning
As a little child, I squealed with delight,
"My Father loves me so much that he is going to teach me to ride a bicycle today!"

Hurry, hurry! I thought, *I must race as fast as I can*
And see the course my Father has set before me!
I looked downtrodden over the course.
"Oh no! It's too complicated to understand! What a mess!" I began to cry.
My Father approached me by my side.

My Father told me that he loved me always and that he was here to stay forever.
And would I accept his help
In doing what I never was able to do myself?

"Oh yes!" I cried, "I'll take the gift!
"I can't get out of this mess I'm in."

He assured me I didn't have to worry.
He'd paid the price,
And then the course was set.

"But how will I make it through the course?" I asked.
"I do not own a bicycle, and I cannot pay."
"Do not worry," he told me. "I already did everything for you.
"I've set the course of your life.
"I'm here to help you."

Lovingly, he helped me ride.
Many times I tried and tried,

But I always failed

Until he gave me yet another gift.

"I overcame for you," he said,
"So I'll help you overcome life's problems—your lingering sins.
"I got the victory for you already.
"Don't you already know?
"I love you more than you can comprehend.
"Now off we go together—always!"

"How could I go wrong with you teaching me to ride today?"

"Just keep your eyes on me and trust," he said,
"And all your doubts will eventually fade away.
"You'll ride that bicycle with me by your side
"To love you, to help you, to be your guide.
"Now off we go!"

And away we flew as he pushed me onward.
And eventually as the day was coming to an end,
I began to cry.

"I still haven't figured it out,
"This mess called life,
"But you have been faithful and true and have seen me through,
"Even when I doubted you,
"Even when I did not trust,
"Even when I took my eyes off of you.
"But I'm so happy that you won my battles for me!"

"You forget the final battle is to ride straight through.
"It's nearly dark," he said.

"I'll help you ride your new bicycle into the garage.
"You can come home now. It's okay!

"I'll help you come inside.
"Just hold on once more!"
He gave a push,
And all of a sudden I squealed with delight!

"I made it through!
"The only way I made it was because of you!
"My loving Father I'll always adore!
"You gave me the gift.
"You helped me through the course!
"The only reason I made it through was because you did it for me!
"That's something I would never have been able to do!

"You helped me repent when I took a wrong turn on my course!
"You steered me in the right direction so that I did repent!
"Oh, thank you for the victories you gave me!
"Oh, thank you for your precious gift. You did what I could not!
"You saved me from my sins, from death!
"You paid the price on the cross for me so that I won't be left outside tonight after dark.
"You adopted me when I accepted your free gift of salvation.
"I am your child!
"I am so excited to make it through so much suffering on this bicycle course!
"The success I had was only because of you!
"The growing pains of falling down were replaced with joy that can't be surpassed.
"On my beautiful day, you helped me through!
"You are my helper through and through!"

"Come on," he said with a smile. "Let's go and enter into my house.
"Well done, my adopted daughter—my good and faithful servant.
"Enter into my joy!"

"Oh, thank you! Thank you!" I said.
"What a day!
"It was hard, but it came to a good end."

The love I had for my Father,
My Father grew for me.
The love I never could fully comprehend,
He grew all along without my realizing it throughout the day on this bicycle course.
While he helped me and I delighted in him,
He grew my love without my knowing—a secret I now realize.
And now I love him even more than I thought!
As I went inside, we laughed together.
I was happy forevermore,
Safe, loved, and comforted.

So here is to the One I love,
My Father, to the one who is in him—Jesus Christ—and to the Holy Spirit.
He will always be with me.
I will always love him through eternity.
Together we will always be!

Scripture Reference: Revelation 22:16
See also parts of the Old Testament and of the New Testament for references to the Trinity.

Out of a Mustard Seed You Came

When my father and mother hurt me emotionally,
When I am rejected by my loved ones,
When the world hates me for the sake of the gospel,
I have the hope of heaven.

When my heart's desires change to match God's will and not my own,
When I lose the desires of my heart for the sake of the gospel,
When my dreams are shattered,
When I lose the life I wanted for myself,
I look to heaven for my future,
And simply put,
I have the hope of heaven.

But how does one attain heaven?
The answer is simple and true.

When I hear the gospel and understand,
When my heart begins to grow,
When I begin to desire the free gift of salvation Jesus Christ offers,
My heart begins to harken unto heaven.

When my heart grows to the point that I desire to accept the free gift Jesus has to offer,
And I want to be counted among those in heaven by Jesus Christ himself,
Out of the desire in my heart to be saved
—to drink of the free gift of the water of life, to accept the free gift of salvation—
Out of this desire my heart begins to turn to the call of Christ through the power of the Holy Spirit.

Finally, when I ask Jesus Christ to be my personal Lord and Savior,

I have received the free gift of salvation and been counted among those in heaven.
I have answered Christ's call.
I have answered the call in my heart placed by the Holy Spirit
—to drink of the free gift of the water of life.
I have now harkened unto heaven.

When I give my life unto my newfound Savior,
I reap a lifetime of love,
And some pain in service too if I'm doing something right,
Though all the while it's possible that I look unsuccessful to the world.

For it is worldly standards that Christianity cannot meet
But only surpass!—a hidden blessing many may miss
When the world thinks Christianity to be a failure.

But whether the world considers you successful or not,
In Christ, you are always a success,
Even when it seems you are not,
Because Christ is loving you
While the world says "You fail!"
He is loving you through your little successes and your little failures too.
Your successes cause you to grow spiritually if you learn to repent of your sins.

And with Christ's help,
You can gain success in repentance of your sins
—that is, turning away from sins that are patterned and prolonged.

The key to this success
Is a little secret I'll tell you.

The key to success is asking Jesus to give you success in repentance.
You can ask Jesus to overcome the sins you are trying to turn away from,
To give you success in repentance because he overcame these sins on the cross.

And if you believe you have received this gift,
God will harvest it throughout your lifetime,
And you will reap the benefits.

The benefits won't look like benefits.
Your success in repentance won't be readily apparent,
But while you are going through trials,
You may be able to look back and see your growth
—your little successes—with a little discernment.

The benefits of a lifetime of repentance seem like the opposite to the world
—that is, unsuccess.
The world sees someone drowning in problems the person can't escape
—no matter how hard that person tries.

But I'll tell you another little secret.
If you ask God to rescue you in time of need, he will!
And God sees every time a person conquers life's problems through him,
Even if that person cannot see it at the time.

As that person grows,
He or she has to call upon God's help a little more or a little less depending on our needs,
To deal with a long-term problem,
Until one day the person is able to say,
"God gave me success in repentance over this issue!"

One marvels at what God has done when this occurs.
One sees the person's success.
But the world will never see someone's newfound victory in repentance,
For the world does not believe in Jesus Christ.

The world hates you for the sake of Christ.
The world rejects you.

Families and neighbors turn against one another, forsaking each other.
And whether they do not realize what they have done or have acted on purpose,
Through emotions and problems loved ones can feel rejected by each other.

Besides suffering for the sake of the gospel,
People may be persecuted by their families for who they are, for their problems,
or maybe even because family members cannot see the little successes God gave them.

And if you do not feel persecuted or rejected for the sake of the gospel close to home,
Through emotional distress caused by the blindness of what your relatives do to you,
Or the hurt they may cause you,
Then it is guaranteed that the world will persecute, hate, and reject you for Jesus's sake.

But you are not of the world, so you believe.
You harken unto heaven's call out of the desire of your heart.
You accept what Jesus did by asking him for the free gift of salvation he offers to everyone,
So that now you are counted among those in heaven.

And even if you lack the confidence to say "I'm definitely saved!" after you asked for salvation,
Where confidence is lacking,
Faith grows confidence in time
To scatter any doubts about whether you truly have salvation.

And even if you die before you find your confidence,
It never changes the fact that Jesus Christ died on the cross for all that you ever did wrong,
A perfect substitution for your sins
So that you do not have to go to hell after you die.

And simply put,
Any lack of faith will never change the truth
That you asked and are therefore saved
Because you asked rightly, out of the desire of your heart, to go to heaven,
A prompting that comes from the Holy Spirit whether recognized or not

And that makes even the smallest of faith valid in God's eyes.

For even the smallest faith—the faith of a mustard seed—is enough to be saved.
And the smallest of faith—even the simplest—may not go unpunished
But ends up being the greatest faith of all.

And even though the world may never recognize your faith,
Because it does not believe in Jesus Christ,
As your mustard-seed faith grows,
You live,
You love God,
You love your neighbor, which is really loving the world that hates you,
You repent,
You see your victories in repentance through discernment,
And you rejoice when you see all the little victories God gave you.

I'll tell you one final secret.
In the Christian walk,
The only way your faith truly blooms
Is through a relationship with Jesus Christ.

Following Christ is all about praying, reading the Bible, repenting,
And following his will!
The key to a good relationship with Jesus Christ is loving him, listening to him,
And putting him first in your life through prayer.

And in prayer one day you may learn to pray without ceasing,
A true gift from God
That draws you more intimately to him.

For Jesus Christ is the only way to salvation,
And even if you doubted that Jesus saved you,
Through your faith, he did.

Jesus saved you when you drank of the free gift of the water of life
By rightly asking him,
Through the prompting of the Holy Spirit,
Out of the desire of your heart to go to heaven,
To have the free gift of salvation.
You asked Jesus Christ to be your personal Lord and Savior.

Now in newfound faith,
Through grace and peace, you go forth,
And in Jesus Christ, you stand.
You harken unto heaven for your future.
Out of a mustard seed you came.

Out of Misguided Love, I Judged Others' Salvation: Please Pardon My Sins

What shall I say and how shall I begin?
My life is full of never-ending sin.

Not always remorseful was I.
Not always was I willing to comply
When it came to the passions in my heart.

What was this deep-rooted passion that trouble did make?
Out of misguided love, my mistakes
Were too many to count.
No mercy was found.

My sin was great.
Out of misguided love, my mistake
Was to judge whether my loved ones did partake
Of the free gift of the water of life.
My sin was to judge whether other people in my family,
Professing to be Christians,
Truly had the free gift of salvation.
I judged whether I thought they had eternal life in Jesus Christ.

Over time I learned
As my heart yearned,
Growing more and more restive.
My heart became unsteady
Out of love for my family.

I desired to see my family again one day
When life's journey was over.

I witnessed and spoke what I thought was true.
And I still believe it is the truth:
If you ask Jesus Christ to be your precious Lord and Savior,
You therefore receive your salvation.
Even if you lack confidence and have doubt, it will never change the truth:
You are saved if you have asked Jesus Christ to be your personal Lord and Savior.
And in asking for the free gift of salvation,
You are prompted by your heart's desire,
A prompting I believe comes from the Holy Spirit.
This prompting and asking are always true
And are a valid way to salvation.
If your heart is sincere in asking for the free gift of the water of life,
Then it will be done for you!
I believe your faith is like a mustard seed
If you ask for salvation
Out of the desire of your heart
Placed there by the Holy Spirit,
But you lack all confidence to say you are saved.

My sin lay in not letting my loved ones go their ways.
Instead their choices I tried to sway.

Persuasive conversation I did try.
Countless years continued to pass me by
As I begged and pleaded.
Oh, how I tried
To tell them to ask Jesus Christ to be their personal Lord and Savior.

Out of your heart's desire,
It is true, not false,

Because it is prompted from within,
A desire planted in your heart by the Holy Spirit,
Who lives with you and within you.

In the form of a prayer, please accept Jesus Christ, and you will have salvation!
I prayed. I tried to tell them. I cried and cried.
It is the truth.
If you believe,
Please do this to make sure you will call heaven your home!

They turned me away and told me time and time again,
In many different ways,
They believed this was false.
They believed I was spreading lies!
I was judging their salvation!

They tried to throw me out of their lives,
Or in the case of one, simply ignore me.
They were tired of hearing me rant and rave.
"You are crazy because of this belief!" one insisted.
"You are spreading false assurance of salvation!" another did say.

But no matter who it was within my family
Whose views differed from mine,
They all seemed to say, "You are wrong. You are lying.
"We won't let our families accept what you say!"

Then one night I realized I was trapped and had judged myself
Into a situation surrounded by lies everywhere—a deep and dark pit.

And then the answer came to me when I wondered why I felt condemned,
As though I had been sentenced to bear something I could not.

The answer came to me but was somewhat unclear.
I had judged others' salvation,
So I was judged.

My punishment is great.
In addition to the emotional torture I bear
Over a family that did not validate
The core of what I am and of what I believe,
I must bear the sadness and the fear
And never know if I will ever see them again
When life's journey is over.

We do not speak in terms that communicate
If we truly have salvation.
Our hearts, in secret, covered over, cannot be shared.
But while in agony,
I am loving them all the more,
Not knowing if I will ever see my family once again.

So what do I do? And how do I cope?
God led me to an answer I did not fully understand.
First, he showed me where I went wrong and what I did.

I sinned in judging others' salvation.
The answer I desired I will never know in this lifetime
Because of their decisions not to discuss the question.
Their choices were apparent from what they did say,
But these choices were just not the same as mine.

By exercising their rights,
They distanced themselves from me.
In torture I go forth
With occasional peace and with grace that the Holy Spirit gives me

So that I may pray and go where God wants,
So that I may continue on.
This is the punishment for my sin,
Life's pain and agony.
Ever mindful about matters of the heart and of eternity,
I sinned out of the desire to gain peace in my heart.
I looked to my family members to see if they would give me
Assurance of their salvation.

What I finally did learn
Is that this assurance can be found only by each individual.
Some are mistaken and have false assurance,
While others know the truth.
It's not my place to judge others' assurance of salvation
But only to worry about my own
And to spread what I believe to be true about salvation.
In doing this, I may help others decide
What they want to believe.

I am not supposed to judge others' assurance of salvation.
I am not supposed to judge whether people are truly saved,
Even if I disagree with their views on salvation.
It is not my place
To judge in this way
Because that is God's job.

If they truly have what Jesus Christ defines as salvation,
Their names will be found in the book of life, and their eternal destination is secure.
In judgment God will examine how they used their gifts and opportunities.
If they are saved,
They will be delivered into righteousness instead of condemnation.

Another thing I learned about judgment

Is that many are quick to judge in anger,
Which is like saying they are without sin,
A hidden lie most people almost always miss.

Trapped in a pit of lies,
We are covered in darkness when we judge others.
The only time we are to judge,
A duty we must not take lightly,
Is when a person's sin hurts others and the person shows no remorse.
We are to discipline that person in love and not to take revenge.

So what do I do and where do I turn
To show repentance for judging others' salvation?

The first step is to acknowledge
That although I acted out of love and concern,
I violated their rights to disagree and to discuss.

Next all I can do is ask forgiveness,
Which I have tried to do in letters to all.
I have asked forgiveness for judging their salvation.
I recognize my heart was in the right place and I was acting out of love.
But in acting out of love,
My heart led me astray.
I must let go.
I must let God lead me to pray
And go where God wants me to go.

And there is one more task I can do,
A task that is hard
And that will take a lifetime.
It's never over until life's journey ends.

The task is this: to show mercy, compassion, forgiveness,
To be their friend.
In being their friend, I am loving them as I love myself,
Even if I cannot share who I really am,

Out of respect for their unwillingness to hear about my faith.
Our differences I must learn to accept.

I must conquer my fear that I will never see them again on the other side
By asking God for peace when I cannot see the answer
And for grace to continually uphold me as I walk through life.
A task he has shown me,
And he gives grace to those who ask the Holy Spirit for help
And who believe the Holy Spirit will help them.
They may not receive grace and peace right away,
But they will receive it when the time is right.

In grace and peace, I am able to continue on
Without all the answers.
In faith, hope, and love,
I pray, I cry, I try.
I do not get angry with God about my family's disagreement over what must be done to be saved.

I must show an interest in my family.
I must put myself aside.
In love I must act
To be the sister they will love.

But in acting in love as time goes by,
A part of me will always feel
Slightly held back
Through love's appeal.

My heart's desire
Is that they will one day ask Jesus Christ to be their personal Lord and Savior.
I have very little hope.

I go forth upheld in grace and peace but at times with much sadness
Because I am not allowed to be true to myself.
I am not being true to myself
When I am not speaking my mind
About my heart's desires
Or talking about what makes me truly happy,
Which is talking about God.

I cannot speak about these matters to family members anymore
Because they have asked that I do not
And because at least one will throw me out of her life forever if I do.

My heart's desire did not change.
Yes, it's still the same
Even if they say, "I disagree! I do not believe you! I do not wish to talk because it is false!"
I recognize that it is their right to do what they want.

If only I could have the peace of knowing I will see them again.
I struggle with this torment,
This lament!
I suffer the curse of worry and of being ever mindful,
Of thinking about where we will end up in eternity.
I am unable to stop thinking along these lines
Because where we go eternally is all that matters in our lives!

I will try to go on loving them for who they are,
To make a few good memories,
To smile a little too hard.

But in love, tormented until I am at peace,
I will never know what I need to know.
It led me to sin,
To judge others' salvation,
To do God's job.

May God have mercy upon me and upon us all
So that when the day of judgment comes,
We will all be clothed in garments of salvation and righteousness,
Fully accepted by God,
Legitimate children, adopted and loved.

So here is to my family.
I am so sorry
I judged your salvation.
I did God's job.

I will continue spreading what I believe in.
It's all I have left to hold on to that is real on the inside.
It's truly a special gift
The Holy Spirit gave me
To desire salvation in my heart,
To ask for the free gift of salvation,
And to encourage others to ask for this gift if this is what they desire.

I want my family members to know
That I will always love them,
Even if I will never know where they stand.

And just because I cannot comprehend,
Or because they do not want to tell me,
So I have little hope,
I may still see them again in heaven one day.

This lack of knowledge and understanding
Makes me feel as though I go out weeping as I carry the seed.
I will return in joy one day, carrying my sheaves!

I don't know if I will see my family again,
But maybe one day
Or after time ends,
I will know for sure
When God shows me the truth.
And when it's all over,
No matter the outcome,
I will finally be at home and at peace.

Scripture References:
1 Corinthians 5:12
Isaiah 61:8–11
John 8:7
Matthew 16:27
Philippians 2:9–11, 4:2–3
Psalm 126:7
Revelation 3:5, 20:11–15, 21:27, 22:17
Romans 5:12

Absent Friends

I'd like to say on every morning of every day
And late upon the eve and every morrow and back again,
Good morning and good night to my absent friends:
My family members who cannot be with me
Through death or by choice,
Through separations because I did once offend,
Through separations that may or may not mend.
Though they may not be able to say they love me,
I love my absent family members—my absent friends.

I say good morning to pictures of perfect days passed,
Days never to be regained.
Love remains frozen on their faces,
But has love remained in their hearts over time?

Though our differences and life's problems get in the way,
Though separations cut the soul, the spirit, and the heart like knives,
They will never be forgotten—my absent family members, the ones I call absent friends.

But although most remain,
They choose to deny me their hearts' love for whatever reason.
So sadness and despair set in,
Yet hope remains that one day, once again,
I will say good morning to my absent friends

And one day things will be on the mend.
They will love me for who I am,
Forgive me once again,
Welcome me in.

Here is to my absent friends,
Even if they never turn back in their hearts and their ways,
Even if they never say "I love you" or "I forgive you" or "Come back into my life,"
Or if they have passed, and I end up never seeing them again.

I can always say good morning and good night to my absent friends,
Even if they are never to be anywhere in sight again.
And I can always love them in my heart for who they are,
For who I know them to be when they last let me in their lives,
Even if they never let me back in.

Here is to my absent friends,
Whom I will always love despite my pain.
Good morning and good night, my precious absent friends—my precious absent family.

To My Father for Whom I Am Grateful

I try to let you know as much as I can
That I love you.
In more ways than I realize,
You have always been there for me
When I needed it most.

Looking back,
I remember the countless times
We shared a Bible story or two,
Sat in front of a fire you made on a cold, rainy day,
Smiled as we ate ice cream,
Made creative projects together.
I could never have done these things on my own.

I hope you will think back and reminisce
And hold your treasures in this box,
The heartfelt cards, drawings, and papers,
Or whatever makes your heart glad.

And know that while I lack the skill to make this box for you,
People never lack the skill
To love a father,
Or others who are important to them,
For who they truly are
Through and through.

Mom, You Mean More to Me

Mom, you mean more to me than words can say,
But I am trying to honor you every moment of every day.
Your company brings joy to me that words can't describe.
You are always there for me when times are hard.
You bring a smile to my face and light the way,
For your love, joy, and harmony brighten my day.

When I tell you I love you, I mean it every time.
So remember one thing I'd like to say:
Thank you for being a true mother through and through,
For loving me, for never letting me go,
For always being there,
And for simply being
My mother.

Always, You Are My Mother

Always,
You are my mother.
Always,
Your smiles brighten my day.
Always,
Your hugs welcome me when I am down.
Always,
You are here to stay.

Always,
I love you more as you get older.
Always,
I know you will see me through.
Always,
Your love will never depart from me.
Always,
I'll be proud that you are my mother.

Always,
You turn stormy days into sunny ones.
Always,
Your love never disappoints,
Even during life's many disappointments.
Always,
I will keep love's memory of you.
Always,
Remember you are my mother,
And always,
You are loved so dearly!

A Personality's Peculiar Dream

In a dream so eerie, my child personality—the I—came alive in the dark of night. In sleep, she shared a terror born of surreal imagination.

Silenced for three days, the I would no longer be still. Her subconscious fears tormented her throughout the night.

Her dream of a timeless realm began. This realm may have existed for an eternity, or perhaps it symbolized what was, or worse, a time that was to be. Perhaps the past met it somewhere, or maybe her dream shared this realm of peculiarity with the place where the past and the future lie. Perhaps the realm of darkness, her biggest fear, would simply disappear!

Childhood memories remained in the realm of peculiarity. Times past were forgotten, but the faces of those so dearly loved still existed.

The I was the child personality from the fall of 1986. Her family had always called her Mandy and still does today. And Mandy she was in this realm of peculiarity.

The memories that remained in others' minds no longer existed for Mandy. She could remember only the faces of those once loved. Though they had vanished from the timeless realm, they eventually would reappear. But some would go their own way, though perhaps for only a little while. No one could know the end in this peculiar realm, for every person's fate is different.

Mandy started her journey slowly. This reflected her character. Her mind was undeveloped, irrational, and too slow for society's tastes. She always lived six months behind the times.

She walked accompanied by her sister, her brother, and her parents. They smiled amid the darkness they had created in argument and depression—a family fate. The children were so young that they did not know which way they would go.

Mandy's parents gave her brother and sister the most attention, showering them with treasures. Her siblings could not comprehend all this love.

As time flew by and darkness fell across the sidewalk, they smiled, they laughed, and they thought of happy times.

Hurry while they do not see! Mandy told herself. *Run somewhere safe. Hurry up on this dark day, and don't delay! Hurry up and run away! Go back to where you just came, the Mandy of 1986!*

At five years old, Mandy did not wish to be forgotten or destroyed by life's peculiar ironies. She could sense bad feelings everywhere she turned. *Hurry so nothing will be amiss. Let's go, let's go, so I will exist!* she thought. Her existence counted above everything. Oh, how happy she would be to stay five years old!

Mandy desired never to forget the love she had for the Lord Jesus Christ, whom her father forbade her to formally accept. She was too young to have this right, he declared, and would have to wait until she was older. Her father let her accept the Lord Jesus Christ formally in prayer years later. Mandy always felt God would come back for her one day. Much to her delight, he remembered her despite her ways.

The five-year-old knew Scripture passages, for they were read to her at bedtime, and she yearned to be in heaven. With the Scriptures ingrained, Mandy realized she must not forget her love for God. In loving Jesus, she developed a deep desire for salvation. She never wanted to lose the Lord Jesus Christ. Fearing this, she was often scared when others walked out of her life.

Mandy ran swiftly, for she did not want to cease to exist. She feared that if this happened, she would never meet the Lord Jesus Christ. Suddenly, running backward, she stumbled upon an unusual hospital.

She entered quietly and looked around, but there was no time to sit down, for she was swept along to a long rectangular desk.

"Do you have an appointment?" the receptionist asked. "Now hold on, wait, and let me see! You are to go to the basement and room three!"

Mandy wandered among the crowds. *What's wrong with these people?* she wondered. *Can't they see? No one's talking to them, or so it seems.*

Pushing her way through corridors, she saw the most peculiar smiles. Doctors hooked up people to large machines. *What's that I hear? What's that I see? The waning lights, the sound of electricity!* Mandy did not know that each room she passed represented the things that were yet to be.

Where, oh where is room number three? she wondered. Mandy panicked. She found the staircase. How it did wind!

Mandy hesitated as she passed the doors on each floor. How frightful those doors seemed! Behind them lay past possibilities and an uncertain future. But Mandy did not age as she hurried throughout time in this most peculiar hospital.

She gave a sigh when she reached the basement. *Oh, finally! Now where's room number three?*

A desk loomed high above her in the dim light, and she saw a receptionist. "Fill out this form," the receptionist said, "and don't delay!"

"What can I do?" Mandy asked, beginning to cry. "I cannot read or write!"

"That's too bad," the receptionist sighed. "I guess we'll have to fill out the forms. But don't you worry; we will explain how your fate will be determined!"

The receptionist hurried around the counter and sat on a chair. Much to Mandy's surprise, she indeed explained the most peculiar form. Did it mean Mandy's demise?

"This is a birth certificate or possibly a death certificate," the receptionist said. "The doctors will determine which one it will be. But time will tell if your personality is frozen or will cease to exist—a fate not to be taken lightly."

The doctors came without delay and quickly concurred. "A birth certificate it will be," one of them said. "Because of your love for God and for others, you will never cease to exist.

"However, you'll have to stay for a time in the blue-lit room, which has no boundaries within. You will face floating demons—octopus in character. Your task is an unusual one. You must beat the demons with a broom and try to make them disappear. But they will never disappear. Instead they will reappear in many forms as they float through ceilings, walls, and floors.

"Your punishment is very great," the doctor said, "but you must know that Jesus Christ is always there. This punishment is temporary and only in life, for one day you will be released to join your parents in love again!"

So Mandy prepared to enter the blue-lit room. Broom in hand, she knew she must make the demons float away and completely disappear—a task too great for any human to complete.

"But do not tempt fate!" the doctor said. "You will lose the One you love, the Lord Jesus Christ, if you die by your own hand and turn your birth certificate into a death certificate. But do not worry. Take solace in your punishment, for Jesus Christ will fight the demons for you and will make them leave you. When time ends, all versions of yourself, all versions of your life, will go to be with your precious One, the Lord Jesus Christ, not because of your punishment but because you believed and accepted that the Lord Jesus Christ would come into your heart and would be your Savior. The sincerity of your ways, whether or not you have the Lord's gift of salvation, determines your fate in eternity. Anyone can be redeemed by Christ's blood merely by accepting his gift out of a desire to be with him in eternity."

With a heavy heart, the receptionist led Mandy to room number three in the limitless realm, a realm without dimensions. Demons flitted about in the blue light; they simply would not fade!

"But here, for now, I will wait, for I am stuck in life," Mandy said.

A stranger one day came to rescue Mandy. He brought her out of the blue-lit room, leaving the demons behind. As the two ascended a winding staircase, the mysterious stranger was by her side, concealing his identity with a cloak. They rushed up the staircase, laughing heartily. Then they raced through the corridors and through the main hospital door.

Finally, finally, I am free! The stranger has won! But who is this man of mystery? Where has he gone? Mandy wondered.

Then she beheld a sight almost too unreal to believe. For at the gates of this peculiarity she saw a shabby adult version of herself, who had despaired after a life of struggles.

As this person stood looking at the five-year-old before her, she slowly remembered her better angel. Behold Mandy, sometimes known as Amanda. Mandy began to take charge. She stepped forward and entered into her adult life as Amanda. Uncertainty then gave way too much surprise, for Amanda again became Mandy, and there her parents were. Her appearance was shabby no more!

Then a miracle took place. We all appeared as we did in 1986. Renewed and strengthened by grace, we went forth down the winding sidewalk. Dawn would soon arrive. Jesus Christ is sometimes called the bright morning star, and on him we set our sights.

We all desired to put our best selves forward. We walked along in hopeful delight, awaiting our Savior's return to take us home, for with Jesus we will press onward until it is our time.

I Am a Rose

I am a rose.
I hope.
I have faith.
I love.
I wait for love to return to me once again—the love of my family.

I live on a fence.
As I grow away from the fence, I become stronger, and I move away from my home.
As I grow away from the fence, many thorns sprout.
These thorns push me away from my resting place—the crack in the fence.
These thorns separate me from my home.

My thorns are destructive.
My thorns tear away at boundaries with family members.
As these boundaries are being torn down, I grow away from the fence—I grow away from home.
As I grow away from the fence and more thorns sprout,
More family members turn away from me in their hearts because boundaries have been violated.
With these boundaries violated, I face persecution for my faith.
I am rejected for my view that if you ask Jesus Christ to be your personal Lord and Savior, he will be.
He gives the water of life to all who ask for this free gift of salvation
—to all those who ask him to become their personal Lord and Savior.
The rose on the fence is watered by the water of life.
The water of life grows the rose lovingly, increasing its faith.
The water of life continues to love those who reject the rose for its faith.
This makes the rose grow more beautifully, increasing its faith even more.
The faith of the rose is plain for all to see.

The faith of the rose is evident when it talks about God's plan for salvation.
The faith of the rose is apparent only because God waters the rose with the joy of salvation —a lasting joy placed in its heart by the Holy Spirit.

With this water, you will never thirst again.
It tastes of a sustaining joy that the Holy Spirit brings to your heart.
It is self-sustaining and it is small, but it is large at the same time.
It is the greatest joy ever known in the smallest, quietest place possible—one's heart.
The faith of the rose leads back to its source—the water of life.

I am a rose.
I bloom when I focus on God's plan for salvation and when love perpetuates me in time.
Faith grows so strong when it receives the water of life,
When I preach the Word of God, and when I encourage others.
When the plan of salvation is preached without regard for personal consequences,
Faith is its strongest, and so are hope and love.
So I'll tell you a little secret:
When faith, hope, and love are at their strongest, a rose's beauty is at its peak!

A Mother's Love

The wind blows cold and threw the air,
A child is born of mother fair,
Like all the children of the earth,
Their mother' love is shown from birth.
Her ardent love ascends aloft!
Her gentleness tucks in so soft.
As whispers tell of times gone by,
With radiant love you can't deny.
A mother's love for child and life,
Though may endure a little strife,
Shall always willingly comply.
And when a child is fully grown,
When whispered winds have fully moaned,
Though mother's love hath ebbed away,
Her love remains in harbored bay.
A sturdy craft within your days,
That sails into the bay of heart,
Though death may come it never parts.
So, mother's love endures once more,
Which always children will adore.

A Taste of Jesus's Perfect Love

Late at night I was still awake, too afraid to sleep,
For death had come knocking at my door.
As I silently wept,
I felt my tongue and my throat begin to swell.
I sat there getting weaker and weaker.
I finally got up to go to bed.
Fear seized me.
When will it end? I wondered.
Is this the end?

As I looked above from my double bed,
I saw demons whirling around and flying overhead.
What perplexity is this? I thought.
I am a Christian, and I am scared.
This really should not be.

The answer came from inside my head
As I remembered Scripture.
I would ask Jesus Christ to be with me,
For his perfect love to cast out fear,
And all would be well again,
No matter where life took me.

But first I asked Jesus Christ to make the demons leave.
He answered—quickly!
I looked around and realized the demons were gone!
He had answered my prayers!
I'd called upon the name of the Lord for help,
And he'd rescued me instantly!

This seemed foreign to me.
Yes, he had always rescued me, but his response seemed much slower in the past.

I had felt the answer to my prayer
And had experienced Jesus's perfect love,
The Holy Spirit, who is with me and in me.
I had felt home.
He is always there, even when I do not feel him.

He's there for me
But deep within,
So at times I do not always realize
Or am not mindful of his presence.

Thinking back upon my past,
I am sorry for all the times
I sinned against God
And against myself.
I did not always realize
This was a sin not only against myself
But against the Holy Spirit.

I felt the Holy Spirit was with me as a cool presence from above,
And then I felt him from within,
The cool mark on my forehead.

I was so happy that God was with me!
He comforted me in what I thought was my final hour!
As my body began to fall asleep
And I settled down,
I stopped weeping.
His strong and faithful presence
Made me realize a secret I did not know before:

That as you die, even if it's not your time, and your death does not occur,
God's perfect love, which casts out fear, is ever present.

Able to gaze into the darkness unafraid,
While looking east for my bright morning star, the one named Jesus Christ,
Ever watchful,
But never knowing the hour,
I tried to stay awake.

As I lay there, I felt heat from within.
I began to radiate outward from my forehead
A power I recognized as the healing presence of the Holy Spirit.
Suddenly I began to think
My death was possibly being reversed.

I am not sure,
And I will not know
Until life's final hour is over and the journey ends.

Lamb's Trip to the Doctor's Office

A scary sight
The car did make!
Oh, Lamb was nervous.
What would it take?
With rosy cheeks
But tears aplenty,
He climbed into the car,
For today was the day,
And he felt much fear.
A doctor's appointment
Was drawing near!

Lamb rode in the bumpy car very fast,
with the wool on his body flying past!
With tearful pleading eyes,
He arrived at the doctor's office at last!

With much fear he entered
To wait his turn.
With shaking legs,
He was finally called into the office to see Dr. Goat.

Dr. Goat winked and gave a pleasant smile.
"What seems to be the problem?" he asked. "What may I help you with today?
"Take a seat and do tell all!
"I'll do my best; I'll give it my all to help answer your questions."

With shaking voice and sobs coming forth, Lamb did exclaim:

"Whatever shall I do? My wool has gotten too thick to manage. It makes me sad. It makes me blue."
"Oh, do not worry," said Dr. Goat with a smile.
"The answer is simply this: Go see the shearer once a week to manage your wool,
And think of good and positive things, for you will be groomed!
"It will be tamed!" Dr. Goat exclaimed.
"Oh, thank you! Thank you, Dr. Goat!" Lamb squealed with delight.

Very satisfied with himself,
Back to his home Lamb did ride.
Now unafraid to visit the doctor again,
Because the doctor had been kind,
Lamb's fear did completely subside.

This short story/poem is dedicated to Mary Lou James at the Oh Baby! store in Baton Rouge, Louisiana.

Hijacker and the Buttons

CHAPTER 1

One bright and sunny day in 1946, the button makers, appointed by God, were hard at work. They made one shiny button after another. Each was placed on its very own swatch of fabric. Some of the buttons began to grow threads. This happened in the first three months of life.

There was one special button. Made of sterling silver like a bullet, he captured the sunlight shining in the room. He was called Hijacker, a name given to him by the button maker. Hijacker beamed like the sun.

Three months after his creation, he was given a white linen fabric with white thread. The fabric was so intricate that one could see the twisting of the threads. A few months later he was sewn onto a beautiful christening gown for an infant. The button makers said he was chosen for this special purpose and would remain on the gown until he grew tarnished and his stitches became loose.

The next thing Hijacker knew he was handed to a young woman and was placed in a bin. He was then taken to a 1946 Ford and was neatly stacked among piles of linen. The lady got in the car and began driving.

All of a sudden Hijacker spoke his first words: "I was born to be a rebel!"

"Oh yeah?" said Afflicted, another button. "We are doomed to sit on a gown in a closet for fifty years until we fall off and are lost. Then we will be in torment forever!"

"I am not going to live like that," Hijacker replied. "Mark my words. I am going to be a free button! You just watch. One day we will meet again."

"Well, I am going to be a holy button," said Boss, another button.

"Oh yeah?" said Ginger, a fourth button. "Does that mean you want cracks in your holes so you can die a martyr?"

"I will but in God's timing," Afflicted said.

"Oh, shut up!" cried Pinky. She was named after the silky pink thread inside her holes. "I dream that one day I am going to be in a beauty contest and I will shine on forever!"

"We ought to form an alliance," Hijacker suggested. "All we need to do is find each other once we have escaped our christening gown and make sure our visions for our lives are achieved. As for me, I was born to be a rebel, and I will get what I want by any means necessary! I do not need a vision beyond what I want or about some God!"

At that remark, Pinky's threads began to get wet, for she was crying. "We have all been given a vision for our lives. After all, Jesus made the button makers and they made us! We all recognize Jesus's voice, and he can guide our lives. Hijacker, join the alliance. You suggested it!"

"I've changed my mind," Hijacker said. "I don't need an alliance, a vision, or a God! I was born to live hard! I don't need you, Boss, Pinky, Ginger, or Afflicted."

All of a sudden the Ford was on two wheels and squeezed between two oncoming cars. Pinky, Ginger, Boss, Afflicted, and Hijacker went flying with the linens. They became mixed up as the woman got into an accident, and that was the last thing Hijacker remembered.

CHAPTER 2

When Hijacker came to, he was the first button on the back of a christening gown in a shop. He noticed Pinky's pink silk had been replaced with white silk as was his thread. Hijacker then heard a woman speaking as she held up the gown.

"It's perfect! It is just what my little Tommy needs for his christening gown this Sunday!" exclaimed the customer.

"It's a shame what happened to the woman who brought the gowns to our shop," the saleslady said.

"What happened?" asked the customer.

"Oh, she was in a wreck. Her car was totaled. She is in a coma. All we can do is pray to Jesus for her to come out of it," said the saleslady.

"I will keep her in my prayers," the customer said. "Now, where were we? Oh yes! I would like to buy this christening gown. It's just beautiful."

"Hey Pinky!" Hijacker said. "Where are Boss, Ginger, and Afflicted?"

"Each of them is on a different gown," Pinky replied.

"I have been sold and will be picked up later in the week," Boss said. "Look for me at the cathedral this Sunday. I'm gonna get loose and become the holiest button ever!"

"Over my broken button!" exclaimed Hijacker. "Even if you get loose, I will make sure that you never become part of an alliance, and you will never be in a beauty pageant, Pinky."

"Oh Boss, thank you for showing me the way! How'd you get so smart?" asked Pinky.

"God created me with a spiritual sensitivity, and for that I am eternally grateful," Boss said.

Ginger looked at Hijacker and said, "Hijacker, I dream of being the shiniest button on an animal coat and of being covered in rhinestones."

"You and Pinky would get along well!" Hijacker remarked sarcastically.

"No!" Ginger cried. "I want recognition and beauty to glorify myself and not some dumb god."

"Ginger, watch your language!" Boss said. "Even if you choose a path away from God's will, you should respect other people's beliefs. I pray that one day you and Hijacker will be drawn to the Lord Jesus. Afflicted!"

"Yes," he replied.

"What do you want to do when you are free?" asked Boss.

"I want to be a martyr for Christ. My holes are beginning to crack, so I don't have much time," Afflicted replied.
"I promise that as soon as I escape I will help you with the vision God has given you," Boss said. "We will form an alliance yet!"
"Well, Ginger and I will make sure that never happens," Hijacker said.
Then he heard the customer again. "Oh, thank you so much!" she said.
The next thing Hijacker and Pinky knew they were placed in a bag and were leaving the store. It was a big world out there, and they were about to enter it.

CHAPTER 3

On a bright and sunny Sunday morning, Hijacker and Pinky found themselves in an absolutely beautiful one-story house built in 1940. The customer, Genevieve, was hurriedly getting ready to attend the service at Grace Episcopal Church. The room Hijacker and Pinky were in had white walls and a raised ceiling with crown molding in the top center. The drapes, made of a sheer fabric, descended and formed a pool of material that fanned out on the floor. On the back wall was a small closet with sliding doors. Opposite the closet a high queen-size bed with a tester; the bed dated from 1890. The carpet was gray. Next to the bed was a table with a beauty box on it.

Suddenly a little girl entered the master bedroom. Her name was Rose and she was four years old. She was dressed for church. The little girl walked over to the nightstand. She opened the beauty box, and it began to play music. Rose then slid open the closet door. Right in front of her was her baby brother's christening gown. Rose touched the gown and caught a glimpse of Pinky, who was shiny because she had been crying. Pinky missed Boss and had lost hope in her dreams. The little girl grabbed Pinky and pulled on her until she came off the back of the gown. Rose danced around the room, holding Pinky tightly. She then walked over to the beauty box and placed Pinky inside. "You are mine! Mine, mine, mine!" Rose exclaimed. "I shall keep you for good luck. and you shall come with me to the beauty pageant next month!"

"Rose!" called Genevieve. "Is that music coming from my beauty box? I have told you time and time again not to play with it! Now come to the kitchen and get your breakfast!"

Rose slammed the beauty box shut, closed the closet with the gown inside, and ran out of the room.

"Pinky!" Hijacker called.

"Oh Hijacker! Isn't it exciting? I am going to live my dream after all!"

"I wouldn't rely on that. What if Genevieve notices you are gone, finds you, and sews you back on? You would have been excited for nothing!"

"Oh Hijacker! How can you be so cruel?" Pinky said. She began to sob.

"Pinky, you can stay here and fulfill your dreams, but I am going to take the rebel's way out! I am not sure I will ever see you again, but I will pass on your regards to Boss," Hijacker said.

"For a rebel you sure have a soft heart!" Pinky said. "I knew there was some good in you after all!"

"What!" Hijacker exclaimed angrily. "I do not have a soft heart! I have a heart of pride, deceit, and rage. I just want to do whatever I wish with a free conscience!"

Suddenly, Genevieve appeared in the bedroom. She opened the closet, pulled out the gown, and took a moment to look it over. She gasped when she saw the second button was missing.

"Rose! Come here now!"

Rose sauntered in with an innocent look on her face.

"Where is the button from this gown?" Genevieve asked.

"I don't know. I didn't touch it!" the little girl lied.

"Don't lie to me!" yelled Genevieve. "Oh my gosh! We're going to be late!"

Genevieve dressed Tommy in the christening gown and put a safety pin in place of the missing button. "Rose, when I look for this button later and I find it, you are going to be severely punished!" she said.

The mother stormed out of the room. The little girl went to the beauty box and retrieved the button. She placed it inside her shoe. She caught up with her mother, and they all left for Grace Episcopal Church.

CHAPTER 4

Around ten on Sunday morning, Genevieve, Rose, Tommy, Hijacker, and Pinky arrived at the cathedral. The church was built in 1890 and had ceilings coming to a high point in the center. All of the wood in the church was mahogany. By the back doors, pipes projected outward toward the congregation. At the front were more vertical pipes. There were beautiful stained glass windows just behind the altar. On the walls were plaques with the names of congregation members who had donated large sums of money to help establish the church. Up front on the left wall was a list of past priests. To the right of the list was the marble baptismal font. It had a towel next to it along with a branch of olive leaves.

Behind the font was the vestry where robes, crosses, the book of the gospel, and other items that were important to the service were stored. On the far-right wall stood a podium where the priest gave his sermon. Along this wall were beautiful stained glass windows. There were six of them in all. In the front center between the podium and the baptismal font, stairs led to the back of the altar. To the left of the stairs was an organ. The choir loft was on the right.

To the right of the choir loft and a little to the left behind the podium were pews. There were more pews in the center of the cathedral. Each pew had a kneeler, and there was a plaque on the end of each row. The plaques were given in memory of the families that had donated to the church. A red carpet separated the two sets of pews and went right up the center toward the altar. The priest would pass through the tall doors at the back of the church at the start of the service.

Genevieve, Rose, and Tommy, accompanied by Hijacker, sat in the front left pews because they were near the baptismal font. Suddenly, the first notes sounded from the organ. The priest entered with the staff of the cross, and behind him were the choir members. They sang "Nearer My God to Thee," and the whole congregation chimed in. After the first two lessons for the day and the reading of the gospel, the priest said, "The candidates for holy baptism may now be presented." He was reading directly from the Book of Common Prayer, which is used to structure not only regular services but special rites such as baptism.

Genevieve stood up and said, "I present Tommy to receive the sacrament of baptism."

Then another woman stood up with her baby, who was wearing a gown with Boss on it. The baby's name was Grace Pigeon. Her mother, Nancy, said, "I present Grace to receive the sacrament of holy baptism."

"Hijacker! Where is Pinky?" asked Boss.

"Pinky is in Rose's shoe!" Hijacker answered. "Rose pulled her off of the dress and put her there so she would not get in trouble."

"Rose, honey," Genevieve said, "please hold Grace for a moment while Mrs. Pigeon opens her prayer book again. She accidentally dropped it, and it was closed when she picked it up."

The priest continued the ceremony, asking, "Do you believe in God the Father?"

The congregation replied, "I believe in God the Father Almighty, maker of heaven and earth."

While Rose was holding Grace, she pulled on Boss. She had decided she needed more of these shiny buttons to play with and to bring her luck. Nancy turned and reached for Grace. As she took Grace back, Rose continued pulling on Boss. Suddenly, he came loose and went flying. Boss hit the priest in the eye and landed in the baptismal font.

"I am being baptized! Isn't this great? I am the holiest button ever!" Boss exclaimed.

Then Boss realized he was drowning. "Help, Hijacker! Help, Pinky!"

"Although it is not in my nature to help others, I'll make an exception this time. Grab hold of the sprig when he dips it into the baptismal font," Hijacker said.

Boss did as Hijacker suggested. Then the priest shook the sprig over the baby's head. Boss went flying out into the congregation and fell into a vent.

Rose's feet got sweaty, and she began to squirm in her shoes. This caused Pinky to fall out of the little girl's shoe, but Rose did not notice.

"Boss!" Pinky cried. "I am coming to get you! I will roll toward the vent, and you can throw me the loose thread from where Rose ripped you off."

Boss threw her the thread, and Pinky began to hoist him up. Boss pulled himself through the grate on the vent and was now in the congregation. He and Pinky hid behind a pew as the service continued.

Genevieve eyed Rose angrily. "Just you wait until we get to the picnic," she growled in a low voice. Rose shrank back. "You will apologize to Mrs. Pigeon, and you will work off the debt for her button, which was quite expensive. I can't believe this! Thirty cents! Almost a day's wages!"

"Hijacker!" called Pinky. "Are you still attached?"

"Yes. I am still attached to the gown. I am the only thing holding it closed. After church, maybe I will free myself. I will remind you that I do not need your help!"

"Nancy, I am so sorry about what happened," Genevieve said after the service. "Rose, I think you have something to say."

"I am sorry. I just wanted to play with the button," Rose said.

"I can assure you, Nancy, that she will work to pay off the cost of the button," said Genevieve.

"Pinky, let's try to go with Hijacker so he can be freed," Boss said. "I know he doesn't want help, but I think if we stick together and find Ginger and Afflicted we may yet form an alliance."

"I agree," said Pinky. "But at least you got your dream. Now that you are baptized and you know so much about Jesus, you are ready to help Hijacker and Ginger come to the Lord. What happened to Ginger and Afflicted?"

"They never got sold," Boss said. "We must get Hijacker and bring him with us to the store."

Pinky and Boss waited and watched as the little girl walked down the aisle to the door. Then the two rolled in front of her. Rose picked up the buttons, put them in the pocket of her dress, and walked out. Her mother was outside waiting for her.

CHAPTER 5

Genevieve, Rose, Tommy, Nancy, and Grace arrived at the campground cookout a little after noon. The sky was beginning to look overcast.

"I don't know if this is going to work out, because it looks like it's going to rain," Genevieve said as she got out of the car with Tommy. "Now Rose, go change into play clothes in the restroom. You are getting only leftovers, which I picked up when we stopped by the house."

"Leftovers! Mommy, please! I want a hamburger and a hot dog. I don't want leftovers!" Rose protested.

"This is part of your punishment for your awful behavior!" Genevieve replied.

"Please! I'll be good! I promise!" Rose cried in desperation.

"It's too late for that," Genevieve said. "Now go and change!"

As Rose left to change she began to wail. She fumbled around in her pocket as she entered the restroom. Boss and Pinky were still there. Rose took them out and put them in her shoe. "You're mine! All mine!" Rose said. Then she left the bathroom.

Rose spotted a great big bear fishing in a nearby river. Suddenly she realized the bear was headed toward Grace. Nancy began to scream, but paralyzed with fear, she did nothing. Rose ran toward Grace. As she grabbed the baby, the bear roared and slashed the back of the christening gown. This sent Hijacker flying onto the riverbank. During the commotion, Pinky and Boss had worked their way out of Rose's shoe. Rose held Grace tightly and raced toward Nancy.

Genevieve was screaming, "Rose! Oh Rose! Hurry. Run to the car!"

"I'm coming, Mommy!" Rose cried.

"Oh Rose! Thank you!" exclaimed Nancy. "You saved my baby!"

Down at the riverbank the bear had picked up Hijacker because he was so shiny. The bear's name was Rocky. "What are you doing here, little button?" he asked.

"You denied me the glory of escaping!" cried Hijacker. "You are nothing but a stupid bear!"

Rocky angrily hurled Hijacker downstream, and he was soon in danger of drowning. The bear looked down and saw Boss and Pinky, who was crying.

"You murderer!" Boss shouted. "Now Hijacker may go to hell because he never accepted Jesus Christ as his Lord and Savior. Pinky and I have been trying to help, and now it may be too late!"

"Oh yeah?" said Rocky. He picked up Boss and Pinky and hurled them downstream.

Boss and Pinky landed next to Hijacker. He was unconscious, and they were beginning to sink. "Oh Boss, what are we going to do?" Pinky cried. "We are all going to drown!"

A dog stepped into the river for a drink of water. His name was Fire the Hazard Dog. The firemen in town had given him this name because he was more likely to start a fire with his bumbling than to fight a fire. A Dalmatian, he wore a red bandanna around his neck and a red fire hat on his head.

Pinky and Boss scooped up Hijacker, and all three of them clung to the dog's fur. When he left the river, he lifted them out of the water. Finally, he looked down and saw them.

"What are you doing here?" asked Fire the Hazard Dog.

"You saved our lives!" Boss told the dog. "We are trying to round up our friends Ginger and Afflicted as well as Hijacker to form an alliance so that together we may follow our visions. As we focus on the Lord and become familiar with his plan for our lives, our visions will change to match what he asks of us."

The water drained from Hijacker's hole. He coughed and then spoke. "Pinky and Boss, you saved my life! But why?" he asked.

"It is what Jesus would do," Boss said, "and because of what he did for you on the cross, Jesus can save your soul and you can go to heaven after you die. But if you do not accept Jesus Christ as Lord and Savior before you die, you will go to hell."

"Well, I am not about to accept him. I am living hard! Yeah!" said Hijacker. "I am living my dream!"

"Is your dream more important than God?" asked Boss.

"I don't know anymore," said Hijacker.

Boss was about to tell Hijacker that God was more important when suddenly Fire the Hazard Dog stopped. A forest fire had broken out in the south part of the campground. The dog decided to run through the fire. Still clinging to the dog, the buttons began to overheat and became hot to the touch, and that was the last thing they could remember before all three of them passed out from smoke inhalation.

CHAPTER 6

It was a dismal rainy day back at the christening gown shop. Ginger and Afflicted remained on separate gowns. It was Monday, the day after Pinky, Boss, and Hijacker had escaped their gowns. Suddenly a young woman walked into the store with two children and began talking to the owner.

"I must have these two gowns for my twins for baptism next Sunday," the lady said.

"I hope they do not have bad luck," the owner said. "I don't know if you heard about two of our gowns yesterday. What a disaster that was! Rose pulled the buttons off the back of Grace and Tommy's gowns! And that's not all. Grace was attacked by a bear at the campsite!"

"Oh, how horrible! Was everybody okay?" asked the customer.

"Rose grabbed Grace and made a run for it. They were a bit shaken up but otherwise okay. Even worse, after that there was a forest fire at the campsite!"

"Was anybody hurt?" asked the customer.

"No. A dog owned by the fire station saved the day. They call him Fire the Hazard Dog because he usually gets trapped in fires or causes trouble. This time, however, Fire the Hazard Dog raced through the burning brush and alerted the firemen, and they put out the fire before it spread to the city."

"Fire the Hazard Dog is a hero!" exclaimed the customer.

"Hey Ginger!" Afflicted said. "Maybe we will get sold and we can find out what happened to Pinky, Boss, and Hijacker. We may yet be able to form an alliance for Jesus! All we need to do is go to the campground to locate Pinky, Boss, and Hijacker."

Ginger and Afflicted knew this because they were listening to the conversation between the store owner and the customer.

"Well, if you ask me, it is stupid to go there," Ginger said. "I could remain on this gown and have a glamorous life."

"Or you could come with me and have an exciting life and possibly get everything you want when we find Boss, Pinky, and Hijacker," Afflicted said.

"Oh, all right, Afflicted. I will help you. It is probably the only unselfish thing I've ever done," replied Ginger.

"My how you have matured!" exclaimed Afflicted.

Suddenly, the sales clerk put the gowns carrying Afflicted and Ginger in a bag. The customer paid and walked out of the store.

CHAPTER 7

On a bright Sunday morning, one week after the gowns carrying Ginger and Afflicted had been purchased, another baptism service was about to take place at the church. The customer, Gwen, had brought her twins, Michael and Matthew.

Following the priest's lead, Gwen said, "I present the candidates, Michael and Matthew, to receive the sacrament of holy baptism."

"Do you believe in God the Father?" the priest asked.

As the priest continued, Ginger and Afflicted noticed a little boy pushing his way toward the end of a pew to see the baptism. As soon as the babies had been baptized, the priest held Michael aloft so the congregation could see him. The priest began to walk down the aisle, and a second priest followed him with Matthew. The first priest kept fiddling with the button with his big thick fingers, and Ginger was coming loose.

Suddenly the little boy stuck his foot out in the aisle and tripped the priest. Ginger went flying as the priest fell. The priest following him tripped over the first priest. As the priest fell, he grabbed the back of the baby's gown and Afflicted popped off. He landed next to Ginger.

The little boy's mother was aghast. "I can't believe you, son! You are truly the spawn of Satan!" she cried in the middle of the church service. "Oh fathers! I am so sorry! Are you okay?"

"We are fine. Are the babies all right?" asked one of the priests.

The babies made no noise as they lay on the floor. The priests picked up the babies and patted them on the backs. The babies started crying and were delivered back to their hysterical mother. She immediately left for the hospital to make sure they were okay.

Ginger and Afflicted were dazed. "Hey Afflicted!" Ginger said. "We are free! But how will we ever find Hijacker, Boss, and Pinky? We are lost forever!"

"O come now, Ginger! Jesus will show us the way! All we have to do is pray," Afflicted said.

Suddenly they heard a noise. It was the vent. Before they knew it, they were sucked in. The air blew them down the corridor and out into the gutter. It was now raining and they landed in the sewer. They heard a frightening quack and were confronted by something quite unusual.

CHAPTER 8

The quacking got louder and louder as the duck approached. "Are you Afflicted and Ginger?" he asked.

"Yes, we are," the buttons replied in unison.

"My name is Sewer the Duck, but you can call me Sew because that is my nickname. Your friends Hijacker, Boss, and Pinky are farther up in the sewer. They keep talking about an alliance of some kind. I will take you to see them."

Afflicted and Ginger rode on Sew's back for quite some time and finally reached their friends. All three buttons were reading a newspaper.

"How did you guys end up in the sewer?" asked Afflicted.

"After Fire the Hazard Dog saved us, he dropped us in the gutter. We met Sewer the Duck, and he took us to the church. We decided to wait till Sunday, hoping you got sold and would show up there. If you had not been at the church today, we would have found our way back to the gown shop. We never expected to see you swimming downstream."

"I can't believe this!" exclaimed Hijacker. "The woman who took us from the fabric store is on life support, and the hospital is going to pull the plug at the family's request!"

"We can form an alliance and pay our last respects," Afflicted said.

"Well, I am not going!" Hijacker said. "I need to be free!"

"Since you are a risk taker, I have a wager for you," Boss said. "Come with us, and if your heart is not changed, you can leave and not be in the alliance. Do we have a deal?"

"All right, deal," said Hijacker.

Sewer the Duck showed them the way to the hospital. As the buttons were about to enter the hospital, they noticed the door was opening and shutting on its own.

"Hijacker, wait!" cried Boss. "You could get killed!"

A deliveryman carrying a vase of flowers came around the corner and walked toward them. The buttons hopped onto his shoes and made it into the hospital safely. The deliveryman placed the flowers on a cart, and the buttons latched on to it.

"This ought to take us to the lady who transported us," Pinky said.

The buttons climbed up onto the vase as the cart began to move. After several stops, they suddenly found themselves being lifted up and placed on a table next to the lady who had been injured in the accident. They managed to move onto her bed.

A nurse entered the room and placed an oxygen mask over the lady's face. The nurse did not notice the buttons because they had burrowed under the covers. After the nurse left, they came out of hiding.

Hijacker looked at the woman, and his heart was filled with feelings he had never experienced before: compassion and love. "You helped make us who we are. I will always love you for that," Hijacker said.

"Why Hijacker! Your old softy!" exclaimed Boss. "Hijacker, God loves you like you love this lady, because he made you. He wants to save you, and you too, Ginger. Do you both understand?"

"Yes," they replied meekly.

"What must we do to be saved?" Ginger asked Boss.

"Repent and serve God," Boss said. "Ask Jesus Christ to come into your life and to be your personal Lord and Savior. Do it now because you are never promised tomorrow. Bow your heads and thank Jesus Christ for giving you the gift of life. Invite him into your lives to be your Savior. Ask him to save you so that your names may be written in heaven. When your name is written in heaven, it is written in the Book of Life. All those found in the Book of Life have eternal salvation, and all those not found in the Book of Life do not have salvation. They go to hell after they die. Accept Jesus now."

"Okay. I will," Hijacker said sheepishly. "I guess I was wrong. I never focused on God's love, so I could not see how much he cares for me, how he delights in me and wants me to delight in him. No more hard living. From now on I'm living for God all the way!"

"What about you, Ginger?" asked Boss

"Hijacker's right," she said. "I did not see the truth for the same reason, although I guess there are many reasons people refuse salvation."

Hijacker and Ginger prayed and received salvation. Just then the nurse returned to pull the plug on the lady's life support. "Quick! Hide!" Boss said.

"But we don't have time!" exclaimed Ginger.

The buttons lay out in the open on the bed. As the nurse adjusted the sheets, the buttons went flying into the water pitcher on the table. The lady stopped breathing as her life support was removed. At the same time, the buttons drowned. Then they found themselves in heaven. They had been sewn on a gown of righteousness forever, in peace, love, compassion, and joy. They had achieved their dream. They had formed an alliance with God.

This short story is dedicated to Mary Lou James at the Oh Baby! store in Baton Rouge, Louisiana, and to Elizabeth Libbers for all of her years of dedicated work sewing christening gowns.

The Hippo Who Was Loved Again

CHAPTER 1

Many animals were tucked away in the swamps; some lay in waiting, and others moved about freely like happy little larks. Gray Hippo would never forget one animal who had changed his life forever. Gray Hippo lived in the swamps somewhere between Baton Rouge and New Orleans, Louisiana. Most people don't think of hippos as living in swamps, but they've learned to adapt over the years. Gray Hippo had spent many sweet years wandering free. Things would have been far different if not for the small and seemingly insignificant friend who swam into his life one evening. Little Hippo was a marvelous character whom many would have dismissed. His growth had been stunted from birth. He was gray, but his coat was much shinier and far more appealing than most.

Gray Hippo's life had not always been as good as it was now. He had been an ill hippo—ill as in ill-mannered and ill-tempered. He had done things hippos should never do, and this had led to his undoing in his early years. Back then, he used to swim to the furthest reaches of the swamp—the dangerous parts—to find cypress knees to eat. Unlike most hippos, he loved to eat cypress knees and to blow bubbles in the muddy water. But like most hippos with bad habits, he had one huge character flaw: He didn't know his hippo creator. He didn't know anything about God. He didn't know him personally or intimately. As a result, Gray Hippo messed up a lot and was often defiant. He swam to the nether region of the swamp even though Papa Hippo warned him to avoid this area because Cunning the Alligator lived there. Gray Hippo did not know Cunning would be his downfall.

Cunning was a large alligator who liked to lead zoo trappers to hippos in the swamps. He had a deal with Oscar, a snake who belonged to Ralph, the zookeeper. Ralph would take a pontoon boat into the swamps and hunt for hippos. Oscar was Ralph's favorite pet, and the zookeeper always encouraged him to lead the way on these expeditions.

"Little Hippo, good to see you!" Gray Hippo said as his friend arrived one night. "How is the weather on your side of the swamp?"

"No time!" cried Little Hippo. "Grand Hippo is dying, and he hasn't accepted Christ!"

"What?" exclaimed Gray Hippo. "That is the most important thing you could ever do!"

"I know," Little Hippo replied.

"Come on, Little Hippo. There is no time to spare! Let's go talk to Grand Hippo before it's too late!"

"Don't forget, Gray Hippo, that it is still Grand Hippo's decision whether to accept Christ. It is possible he won't believe that there is such a thing as the Book of Life."

"I know," Gray Hippo said.

"Or that if you ask Jesus Christ to be your personal Lord and Savior, he will do as you ask."

"That's right, Little Hippo! Sounds like your faith needs a little uplifting this time. I may be old, but I can still be hip! It's time to put the fruits of the Spirit to use! It's time to use our evangelism skills!"

"It's time for faith busters!" the two of them said in unison, for they had had a long relationship and enjoyed evangelizing and spreading the Word of God together.

They swam out of the little cave mouth where Gray Hippo lived and headed for Grand Hippo's home on the other side of a black tar ravine in the swamp. Gray Hippo did not tell Little Hippo he was scared to go because that black tar ravine had once led to his undoing.

CHAPTER 2

As Little Hippo and Gray Hippo continued their long swim to reach the black tar ravine, night passed into early morning and then into sunrise.

"Look, Little Hippo! Look at that sunrise! Isn't it glorious the way God made that sunrise? Just a few hippo years ago, I think like that. Remember?"

"Yes, I remember when I met you. You had just made it to the swamp via the wildlife rescue advocates who found you wandering the streets after you escaped the zoo."

"And they advocated for me long and hard! 'Save the hippos!' That was their slogan. 'Let the hippos reside in their natural habitat. Don't make them live in captivity. Let them be free.'

"I escaped by playing coy. I was blowing bubbles in the water in my cage at the zoo, and I wouldn't come near the zookeeper when he coaxed me. The zookeeper thought I was cute. And I was! He got nearer and nearer. I just kept blowing bubbles, and he left and returned with two other zookeepers. They started snapping pictures of me blowing bubbles. What a nightmare that was! The flashing lights scared me, and I charged at them. They ran, and I kept running straight out of the zoo. The tranquilizer darts kept whizzing by me, and people were running about in a panic. When I made it out of the zoo, I did not know where to go. I hid behind a Dumpster. Boy that was stupid. That was like an elephant hiding behind a bush. While I was in captivity, I felt unloved but did not realize just what I was missing until I experienced the love of God through others. And that did not happen until—"

"Until faith busters were created!"

"Now I know you are getting excited, Little Hippo, but faith busters would never have been created if it hadn't been for Milly, the animal rights activist, who was called by a scared and concerned citizen who spotted me behind the Dumpster. Milly put me in a temporary home and bandaged the wounds I suffered when I escaped. Once I had healed, she released me into the swamp where there were plenty of animals, including hippos, and that was where I met you when I was out and about one day."

"Gray Hippo, you forgot my favorite part. How did Milly get you to create faith busters?"

"Milly got me to create faith busters—a name I know you appreciate—by telling me about who Jesus Christ was, about how he was with the Father, Yahweh, in the beginning, and about how he loves me. I came to believe in Christ and realized he loved me. I also came to feel the love Milly had for me and to understand what love was by the way she treated me. Milly stressed how important it was to ask Jesus Christ to be my personal Lord and Savior so I could have salvation in his name and to encourage others in their walk with Christ. She talked about conquering obstacles on my faith journey and said anything that might set me back could be corrected through the encouragement of others and by putting the fruits of the Spirit to work. Milly said these problems simply needed a little 'faith busting.' Hence she coined the term *faith busters*."

"I am so glad you told me about faith busting, Gray Hippo. I know it gives you a sense of purpose."

"That's true," Gray Hippo said.

"Look up ahead!" Little Hippo said.

The two hippos saw a vast expanse of black tar oozing out of the muddy swamp. Little cypress knots were visible in the water. Gray Hippo recalled the temptation that caused his captivity during his wild days. He closed his eyes and shed a tear as he and Little Hippo approached the black tar ravine. Little Hippo did not notice that his friend was crying. Gray Hippo tried to erase the horrible memory of that day when he wanted to try the forbidden fruit—the cypress knees covered with black tar—and of how Oscar and Cunning worked toward his demise. It was a nightmare he did not want to think about, and he was glad it was behind him.

CHAPTER 3

Once they reached the black tar ravine, Gray Hippo composed himself and became cheerful as he thought about how he would witness to Grand Hippo. He worried that Grand Hippo might not accept Christ, for he was a wise hippo who lived hard and had never been brought into captivity. The important thing was that they witnessed to him. The rest was up to Grand Hippo.

The swamp was quiet at first, but as they crossed the ravine Gray Hippo and Little Hippo began to hear a low humming noise.

"Little Hippo, what is that noise?"

"I don't know."

They tried to ignore the noise, but finally they caught sight of the source. It was a pontoon boat.

"There! Over there!" hissed Oscar, who was coiled around Ralph's arm. The zookeeper felt Oscar squeeze him and saw the snake point toward the hippos.

"Well look here!" Ralph said. "It's my lucky day! Two hippos! It must be a momma and a baby. Quick, Oscar! Let's signal our team. Let's catch them. What a great addition they would make to the zoo!"

The hippos' heads lurched in Ralph's direction. They saw him and began to panic.

"Swim faster, Gray Hippo! We've got to get away from Ralph and Oscar!" Little Hippo said.

Just then the hippos heard a chomping noise behind them. It was Cunning the Alligator, hot on their tails. Gray Hippo and Little Hippo swam straight ahead, dodging the cypress knees, and then wildly in all directions as a fleet of pontoon boats led by the alligator pursued them.

"Quick, Gray Hippo! I see a cave over there."

"Isn't that Grand Hippo's residence? We don't want to bring trouble to him in his old age. That could hurt our witness."

"You're right, Gray Hippo. Look over there. That cypress tree has a thick vine hanging from a branch."

"Oh, I knew God would rescue us, Little Hippo! I prayed for the answer. Let's grab the vine with our mouths. When Ralph and his team follow us, we will swim in a circle and tie him up."

Gray Hippo and Little Hippo did just that. When they reached Ralph, the other pontoon crews had to stop to help untangle him. Then the sky opened up. The disgruntled zookeepers reluctantly decided to retreat to escape the heavy downpour.

"He did it, Gray Hippo! Oh yeah! God provided a way and he rescued us!" Little Hippo shouted.

The two elated hippos swam to the entrance of Grand Hippo's cave. As they approached Grand Hippo, Gray Hippo got nervous, for he had never been around a dying hippo before. He felt that witnessing to someone who was dying was a test of his courage and faith. It would take everything he had to muster the courage to speak.

CHAPTER 4

"Grand Hippo," Little Hippo asked, "have you ever heard of Jesus Christ?"'

"Yes," Grand Hippo replied, much to Little Hippo's astonishment. "I heard about him a long time ago. I had a lot of fear in my life, and I was filled with remorse and regret. I could not bring myself to accept him, because I felt I did not deserve salvation or forgiveness. That's because I murdered another hippo in my youth. I never intended to kill that hippo. I led him to Cunning in exchange for some delectable cypress knees, and Cunning ate the hippo. I blame myself. How could God ever love someone who takes bribes, steals, and murders?" asked Grand Hippo.

"That's easy," replied Little Hippo. "He died for everything you ever did wrong, no matter what it was, and he offers you a gift—to spend eternity in heaven, to live with him forever, rejoicing in the gift he gives you. All you have to do is bow your head and ask Jesus Christ to come into your life and to be your personal Lord and Savior, and he will write your name in the Book of Life. Then you will have eternal life in his name. You will be counted among those in heaven if you ask him to do that. In short, you will receive salvation. All you have to do is ask."

Gray Hippo was ashamed because he had been hiding his feelings for so long. He felt remorse for his sins but could not get past his doubts. He could no longer contain himself and started to blubber.

"I feel like my faith is inadequate, like I am not good enough, and I feel unloved!"

Little Hippo and Grand Hippo looked at him in shock.

"Of course you're good enough," Grand Hippo said. "You didn't do as many bad things as I did!"

Little Hippo looked at Gray Hippo and said, "God loves you, remember? Milly loved you, Gray Hippo. Her love for you taught you that God loved you and showed you how. When others are loving you, encouraging you, and trying to help your faith grow, they are being Christ to you. That's what it's all about! Gray Hippo, you must not be so hard on yourself. You must forgive yourself. There are people out there who will show you the love of Christ and who will help you and will encourage your faith to grow. Find them and surround yourself with them."

"You are right, Little Hippo. I feel much better," Gray Hippo said.

"Well, it looks like I missed out on a true treasure of life," Grand Hippo said. "It looks like I missed out on the point of living!"

"Your life may have been different, Grand Hippo, but Jesus offers forgiveness and salvation to all. Please accept him before you die so you don't go to a place of eternal torment and fire! He paid the price so you don't have to go there. Please accept!" Little Hippo urged.

"Okay," Grand Hippo said faintly. "Heaven sounds nice."

So Grand Hippo prayed following Little Hippo's lead and accepted Christ. After a little while, they left Grand Hippo to rest and started to swim back to their part of the swamp. On their way home, Little Hippo and Gray Hippo couldn't stop grinning and talking about faith busters.

"Oh, you lift me up!" Gray Hippo sang. "You lift me up, Little Hippo! You encouraged my walk of faith and made me feel better!"

"That's what friends are for," Liittle Hippo said. "I am glad you are reminded of Christ's love and feel loved again!"

"Thank you for reminding me, Little Hippo! I not only feel loved again, but I believe that encouraging others really does help their faith and that you made a big difference in my life!"

"Thank you," Little Hippo said, beaming.

"You're welcome," replied a happy, loved Gray Hippo. From that day on, he went forth always forgiving himself, feeling loved, and encouraging others in their faith.

"Faith busters forever! Right, Little Hippo?"

"Right!" Little Hippo happily agreed.

Evangelizing Hippos Go to the Alamo

CHAPTER 1

"Yeah ... Uh-huh ... That's right, Bill. I am going to get those two hippos if it's the last thing I do!" exclaimed Ralph. "So when do you think we will go back to the swamps to try to nab those tricky hippos? ... Uh-huh ... Tomorrow, you say? Good. This time I want twice as many pontoon boats. I want to go out at sunrise, and I don't want to leave until dusk! Got it? I want those hippos in the zoo! Just think of the money they'd bring in! Considering how they wrapped me up in vines, I think they are smart and could be trained. Those hippos are exactly what our zoo in New Orleans needs ... Yes. That's great, Bill! Give my love to Ida ... Uh-huh ... Okay. See you tomorrow! Goodbye."

Ralph ended the call with his fellow zookeeper, satisfied he had a good chance of catching Gray Hippo and Little Hippo. The next day, Ralph headed out for the swamps. He knew he had a long day ahead of him. He would scour the entire swamp area between Baton Rouge and New Orleans. He knew it would be a tough task. "But someone's got to do it!" Ralph muttered as he prepared the pontoon boat.

"What's that, Ralph?" asked Bill. "What did you say?"

"Oh, nothing, Bill. I'm just thinking out loud. I've got to catch those hippos. I want our zoo to be a success, and it would be a huge success with those two hippos in our collection of trained animals."

"I know," Bill said as he checked the fan on the back of the boat. "Do you have the truck ready to go? When we catch them, we want to be able to transport them to the zoo."

"Yes," Ralph replied. "The truck reminds me of an armored car, and I think of all the money those hippos are going to bring in to our zoo!"

After checking a few more items, Ralph, Bill, and their fleet were off to catch Little Hippo and Gray Hippo. The two hippos did not know they were about to experience the adventure of a lifetime.

CHAPTER 2

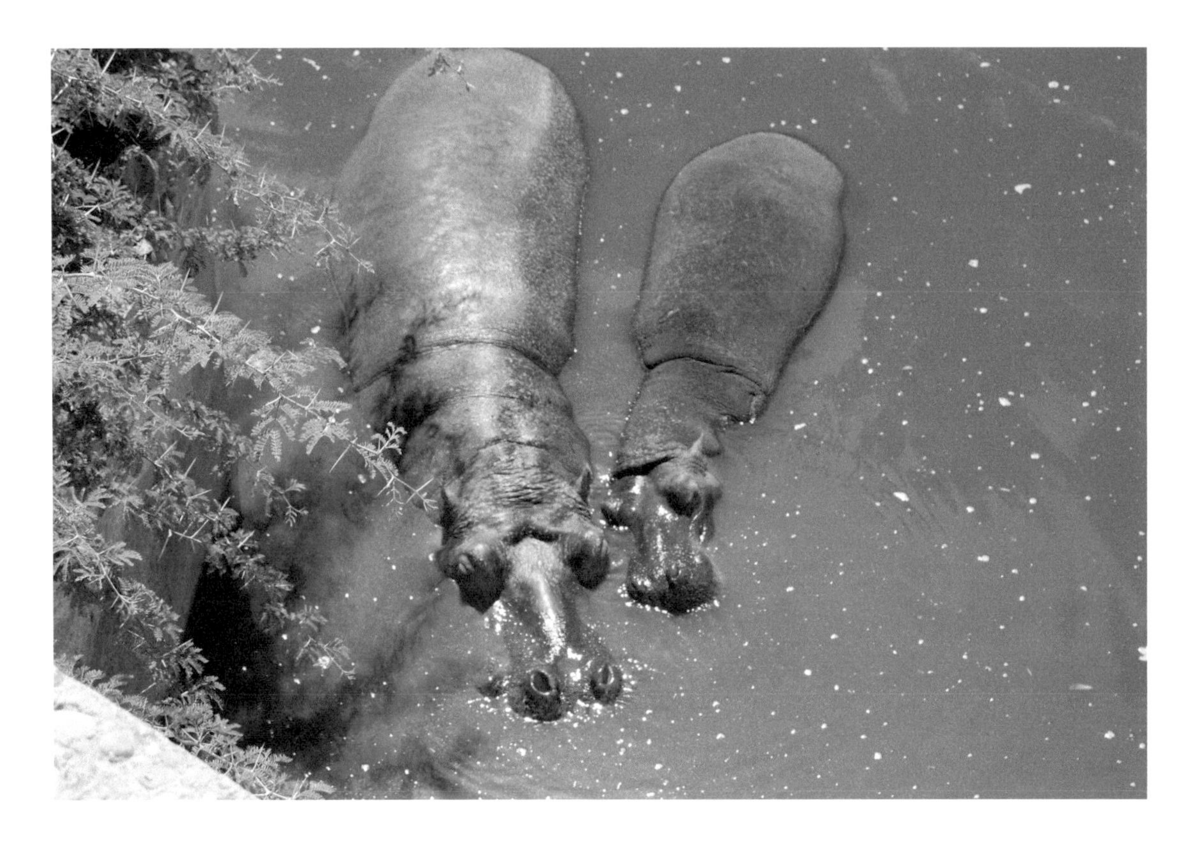

"I am a free, loved, and wonderful hippo!" Gray Hippo told Little Hippo as they swam back home from Grand Hippo's cave.

"Our faith is alive as long as we evangelize and encourage others, love others, and help others grow in their walk with Christ!" exclaimed Little Hippo. "That was great, Gray Hippo! It was wonderful and exhilarating to share the Word of God and to see someone repent and come to Christ! What a life! Right, Gray Hippo?"

"Right!" Gray Hippo agreed. "Oh, look over there, Little Hippo! Water is rushing around the cypress knees!" He began to drool. "That would make them so tender and delicious!"

"Gray Hippo, we can easily find good cypress knees to eat by our home. This is the edge of the black tar ravine. We need to swim further home. It is dangerous out here. Cunning and Oscar could be lurking, and so could Ralph."

"Oh come on, Little Hippo. You're no fun. What's the harm in stopping for just a brief while to be refreshed with the tastiest cypress knees?"

Little Hippo eyed the cypress knees and saw they were indeed tasty looking. Unable to withstand temptation, he said, "Oh all right, Gray Hippo, but only for a brief while."

As the two hippos started to eat the cypress knees, they found these delicacies did not come up out of the water as easily as other cypress knees. This meant that it took the hippos longer to eat fewer cypress knees. A few minutes turned into a few hours, and finally the sun was going down. Gray Hippo and Little Hippo were full of cypress knees and were extremely satisfied and happy.

Meanwhile, Ralph, Bill, and the pontoon boats were still on the prowl, nearing the hippos. "Don't you think it's time to turn back now, Ralph?" asked Bill.

"I will turn back, but give me about thirty more minutes," Ralph replied.

"But Ralph, if you wait that long and we catch them, we may have trouble getting them to the transport truck," Bill said.

"I know, but it's worth the risk. I've just got to catch those hippos. They are going to make our zoo famous!" Ralph said. "Look there! I see those two hippos lazing about up ahead. Quick! Let's sneak up on them. We'll get all the pontoon boats to circle them, and we'll cast our nets. The holding boat is approaching our fleet, and when it arrives, we can lift the hippos with a crane, put them on the boat, and take them to the transport truck. Come on, let's go!"

Ralph, Bill, and the pontoon fleet did just that. They caught the hippos, put them on the holding boat, and transferred them to the truck. When Ralph approached them, the hippos were napping after their big meal, and the first thing he did was shoot them with a large tranquilizer gun. Once inside the truck, the groggy hippos finally began to wake up. They realized that they were moving and that it was dark. They overheard Ralph on his cell phone as he drove the truck.

"What? You mean Bill and I did all of that work for nothing?" Ralph said. "You mean we have to take these hippos to the zoo near the Alamo? That is a long drive! You are going to have to pay us overtime! You are a fool! They could have made our zoo famous! … How? Did you see the way they trapped me the first time I spotted them? They took a vine that was hanging from a cypress tree and swam in a circle when I approached in my boat, tying me up … I'm the fool for letting them tie me up? Well you are going to have to find someone else to transport them! … What? Why would you call Milly?" I thought she was an animal rights activist … She takes care of special protected creatures? And what they did qualifies them as special creatures? Oh, that's rich! … Fine … Okay, bye."

Ralph ended the call and told Bill about the change in plans. Bill froze with a look of terror, and sweat poured down him face.

"Ask … Jesus … Save …" they heard from the back of the truck. Then they heard the muffled words again. "Ask … Jesus … Save …"

"Did those hippos just witness to us?" Bill asked in disbelief.

Ralph, equally perplexed and frightened, said, "I … I think so. Bill, call Milly and tell her the news."

Although he had not fully processed what had happened, Bill did as Ralph asked.

CHAPTER 3

Before Little Hippo and Gray Hippo knew it, morning had arrived. But they did not realize they had been traveling for two days and not one. It was now the second morning of their adventure, and they had arrived in San Antonio, Texas, near the Alamo.

"Just a little bit longer and we'll be at the zoo, Ralph," Bill said. "Shouldn't we be meeting Milly?"

"We are going to meet Milly, Bill. We have to stop at the Alamo to meet her."

They pulled into the Alamo site. Dozens of tourists were lined up to visit the historic landmark. Gray Hippo and Little Hippo looked out of the back of the truck to try to see the old mission for themselves.

"Look, Gray Hippo," Little Hippo said. "It's the Alamo! My dream has come true, and I'm going to evangelize in new places! Come on, Gray Hippo. Help me get out of this van. If we both ram the back of the van, maybe the doors will give way."

The two did just that and the doors flew open. They burst forth and started running for the Alamo. The people in line panicked and scattered as the hippos raced toward the site.

"Gray Hippo, we have to stop running!"

"Why, Little Hippo?"

"Because there is no road ahead."

"Oh no!" cried Gray Hippo.

The hippos tried to stop running but went into a skid. Just before the road ended, they were able to stop. People were still running and screaming, and the hippos began to cry, "Ask … Jesus … Save! Ask … Jesus … Save!"

Then they saw someone approaching. It was Milly.

"Hello, Gray Hippo," she said. "It's nice to see you again. Hello, little fellow. What's your name?"

Little Hippo just barely managed to respond.

"It's nice to meet you, Little Hippo. Now come along with me, you two. I will protect you from the zoo. I am going to make you a petting zoo exhibit at a church in Pigeon Forge, Tennessee, and you will have elaborate cages and get to tell everyone who passes by 'Ask … Jesus … Save.' Got it?" The two hippos grinned.

"Gray Hippo, this is a dream come true! We will be able to witness all day long and live in luxury for the rest of our days."

"Sounds good to me," Gray Hippo said. "Let's go with Milly. But keep in mind that we hippos are escape artists, and I reserve the right to escape her exhibit if I get tired of it or I don't like it!"

"Okay, Gray Hippo," Little Hippo said with a grin. "Thanks for being a friend and for sacrificing your dreams to help me share the gospel. What a life it will be! We will get to witness every day! Faith busters forever, Gray Hippo!"

"Faith busters forever, Little Hippo!" The two hippos smiled at each other and at Milly, and they followed her to the transfer truck, happy and excited about their new life in Christ.

Pigeon Forge, TN: Evangelizing Hippos at the Noah's Ark Exhibit

CHAPTER 1

"I love Jesus! Oh yeah!"

"Sing it to me, Gray Hippo!"

"I love Jesus, and Jesus loves me!"

"Give me a jump and stomp, Gray Hippo!"

Gray Hippo leapt up in the transport van headed for Pigeon Forge, Tennessee, and came crashing back down to the floor, rocking the van side to side. This caused the van to swerve out of its lane and nearly run into a car in the next lane. Milly, who was driving the hippos to Pigeon Forge as a way to spend time with them before having to say goodbye, began to panic.

"Hippos! Gray Hippo and Little Hippo! You two need to settle down back there. You almost caused me to get into a wreck."

"Oh, sorry," muttered Gray Hippo. After that, the only thing Milly heard was the usual noises hippos make. The only words in English anyone had ever been able to make out from the hippos were "Ask … Jesus … Save."

"A true miracle," Milly said softly. She didn't realize she had spoken those words right after scolding the hippos for being rambunctious. Gray Hippo and Little Hippo heard her but were a little confused and sad that she would be so unkind to them.

"This is not like her, Little Hippo," Gray Hippo remarked.

"Even so, Gray Hippo," said Little Hippo, "you don't know the reason she said that. Whether what she said was deliberate or accidental, you have to forgive her for hurting you, even if she won't apologize, because if you don't forgive Milly you won't be forgiven by Jesus Christ. Forgiveness is as plain as that."

"Thanks for reminding me, Little Hippo. I needed that encouragement to do what is right. Hey, Little Hippo, faith busters forever, remember?"

"You are right, Gray Hippo, encouraging others to forgive in an uplifting way might be a good example of using the fruits of the Spirit. I never thought of it like that before. Faith busters forever, Gray Hippo!"

The hippos asked Jesus to consider Milly forgiven, and they silently forgave her for hurting them. Meanwhile, unaware of any of this, Milly glanced at her side mirror and noticed a panicked-looking driver. The driver was odd. He wore lots of jewelry, a hat, and a mink coat in the summer heat. His car had gold accents on it. He dropped back behind Milly's van. She did not realize they were being followed by this mysterious man, a wealthy entrepreneur who invested in expensive things to make money.

CHAPTER 2

"Well, hippos, we are finally here after two days of driving!" Milly said. "Isn't this exciting? I'll get you out of the back, and you can meet your new owner, Rosco."

"Guess where you hippos are? The Noah's ark play in Pigeon Forge!" exclaimed Rosco in his heavy Mediterranean accent. "And guess what else? You are going to star in the production!"

The hippos looked at each other and grinned.

"That's right, hippos. You are going to walk out on stage and board our pretend ark with the rest of the animals, and you'll be featured in our outside zoo exhibit!"

Suddenly the hippos saw the wealthy entrepreneur approaching, and their excitement soon turned to shock and bewilderment.

"How much for the hippos?" the man, named Zeb, asked Milly and Rosco.

"Excuse me?" Milly said.

"What? They are not for sale," Rosco said. "I am the owner now, and they are part of a Noah's ark exhibit. We won't stay in Pigeon Forge forever, though. We travel across the country."

"Forgive my rudeness," the man said. "My name is Zeb. I tell you what, Mister … uh?"

"Rosco."

"Rosco. I will buy a ticket and come to your first performance. I arrange the sale and purchase of expensive things all over the world, including animals." Zeb glanced at the hippos, who drew back and looked sad. Then Zeb looked at Milly and Rosco and continued. "As I was saying, I will buy a ticket and come, and we shall see if your hippos cooperate. I find that hippos can be dangerous creatures unless they are babies. These two are quite rambunctious. I know because I saw the van tilting and swerving. It almost hit my car on the way over here."

"Wait! You followed us?" a shocked and angry Milly said.

"Yes, I'll admit it wasn't very honorable, but when I see something I want, I pursue it," Zeb replied. "As I was saying, if your show doesn't work out, and you want to reconsider selling your hippos, I will be waiting by the petting zoo after the production, Rosco, and you can talk to me. Please be courteous. Even if the answer is no, please come talk to me."

"I am sure the answer will be no," Milly said angrily.

"The answer may or may not be no," Rosco said. "If the hippos are trouble, I may want them to go."

Zeb rubbed his hands together with a look of delight on his face.

"Rosco, if you can't handle the hippos, please let me take them to a hippo retirement farm in the wildlife habitat," Milly said. "I brought them here instead of there only because they are remarkable hippos. They actually say the words "Ask … Jesus … Save." Even if they don't work out in the show, surely you will let them preach from their habitats."

"I am afraid not, Milly," Rosco said. "Hippos are expensive to feed, and I can't afford to feed hippos that don't work for their feed."

"If they don't work out, please release them to me," Milly said.

"I'll consider your proposal and Zeb's," Rosco said.

"Think about where the hippos will be happiest, Rosco" Milly said. "Mr. … uh—"

"Zeb."

"Mr. Zeb, what do you plan to do with the hippos if Rosco sells them to you?"

"I plan to take them to the Audubon Zoo in New Orleans for exhibition. I hear they have a good program!"

"Wait!" Milly said. "You were sent here by Ralph or Bill to try to get the hippos for the zoo. It was Ralph's dream to have them there! Now I know you should not sell to this man, Rosco. He's up to no good!"

"Honestly, Milly, I don't see how sending the hippos to the Audubon Zoo in New Orleans would be bad for them, but I will still consider the habitat idea."

Frustrated, Milly fell silent. She had to help her hippo friends get a home where they would be happy.

"Gray Hippo, Milly still loves us! Maybe she just misspoke when she said it was a miracle that we were quiet."

"Who cares why she made the comment, Little Hippo? Milly did not turn her back on us in her heart! And that reminds me that Jesus Christ will never leave or forsake those who accept him as their personal Lord and Savior. Those who ask Jesus to be their Lord and Savior ask him to take control of their lives and to rule over them. To ask is to drink of the water of life. To drink of the water of life is to obtain eternal salvation in Jesus Christ! See, Little Hippo? I am practicing my witnessing skills! Oh yeah! Faith busters!"

"Good for you, Gray Hippo! I am glad to hear it! Faith busters forever!"

Suddenly the hippos found themselves being led away to their habitat. The big performance was set for that night, and everything hinged on it. The hippos' future was uncertain, and how they acted would determine their fate.

CHAPTER 3

That night, people poured into the auditorium and found their assigned seats. A mother and her daughter sat in the front row a little to the left of the center.

"I'm so glad we're here for the production, Mommy! I'm so excited!" Sarah exclaimed. "I get to see all of the animals!"

Yes, dear," Sarah's mother, Honey, said. "Now you need to settle down. Sit down in your seat and stay seated, young lady! The show is about to start!"

"But Mommy, I want to see the animals!"

"No, Sarah!" Honey said. "If you don't sit down I am going to punish you when we get home. Do you understand me?"

"Yes, Mommy," Sarah said, settling into her seat.

The house lights went down, the curtain went up, and the play began. All was going well until the animals came out right before the intermission.

"Hippos!" Sarah cried with delight as she saw them take the stage.

"Sarah, be quiet!" Honey said in a loud whisper.

"Hey look, Gray Hippo. I think that little girl likes us," Little Hippo said.

"Mommy! I want the hippos!"

"Sarah!" Honey exclaimed so loudly that people began to murmur.

"Well, Little Hippo, maybe we should start telling her about Jesus. I always love to witness."

"No, Gray Hippo. You heard what Milly, Rosco, and Zeb were talking about earlier. We'll lose our homes for witnessing!"

But before he could hear, let alone process, what Little Hippo had said, Gray Hippo found himself bellowing out "Ask … Jesus … Save … Ask … Jesus … Save" in the middle of the play.

The audience got quiet. Suddenly a parrot that was boarding the replica of Noah's ark screeched, "Bad hippos! Bad hippos!"

The audience's murmurs got louder, and the chaos grew as Gray Hippo loudly repeated, "Ask … Jesus … Save." The curtain dropped, and Rosco addressed the crowd over the loudspeaker.

"Attention, ladies and gentlemen. May I have your attention? We are experiencing technical difficulties. We will resume in fifteen minutes."

Milly rushed toward the hippos in tears after the curtain went down.

"Oh, you hippos!" she exclaimed. "Your love for Christ just cost you your home! But don't worry. I will try to do right by you, and I will take care of you if I can save you from that no-good Zeb."

"Now wait a minute!" said Zeb, who had also come backstage. "I am not up to no good! The Audubon Zoo needs money! The hippos can do whatever they want there!"

"No, they can't!" Milly said. "What if they cause chaos at the zoo? Just look at the commotion they have caused here tonight."

Zeb stopped cold and looked down at the floor. He regretted trying to get the hippos for Ralph and Bill. Zeb repented in his heart. He did not want to take the hippos. "Look, Milly," he said. "I am sorry, you are right."

"What?" she asked in disbelief.

"I know you are right. A habitat is the right choice for these hippos. If it were just me looking to buy, I would walk away now, but unfortunately I was hired by Ralph and Bill to retrieve the hippos for the Audubon Zoo. I knew Sarah and Honey, and I made sure they knew about the play. I also knew their tickets were for tonight. I am so sorry, Milly, for the wrong I've caused. I set you up.'

"What?" Milly said. "How dare you come here and try to snatch these hippos!"

"Milly, please don't be angry. I am really a good guy at heart. I may not look like it because of the way I act or maybe even the way I dress, but you have judged me to be a bad character, and for that you are wrong. You should never judge another person in your heart, because there might be something you don't know or see in that person, and judging would be a mistake."

"You are right, Zeb. I have been wrong, and I am sorry. Will you forgive me?"

"Yes, Milly. Now help me figure out something I can tell Ralph so he will not be angry when I don't come back with the hippos. You know what? I should be honest. I will tell Ralph how I followed you and set you up, but I will also tell him I could not in good conscience bring the hippos to the Audubon Zoo, because I was afraid of chaos and danger to the public. I will describe what happened."

"What is going on here?" asked Rosco.

"Zeb and I are making peace," Milly said.

"Ah, that is good. In that case I will arrange to send the hippos with you Milly to their dream retirement home, a luxurious hippo habitat."

"Thank you," said Milly with tears in her eyes.

"Now come on," Rosco said. "We have only ten minutes left, and we need to get all of the animals in their cages so we can perform act two."

"Thank you so much, Rosco, for doing the right thing and releasing the hippos to me," Milly said.

"You're welcome."

The play continued without incident, and the audience went home. Bright and early the next morning Milly rose and went to the Noah's ark exhibit. As she was loading up the hippos, she said, "God did it, hippos! He made a way and caused Zeb and I to repent of our wrongs. God made it possible for you to go to a hippo habitat that is natural and without a cage. Isn't that great, hippos?"

"That's great, Little Hippo!"

"I know that's great, Gray Hippo!"

The two hippos were so happy about having a new home that they wanted to celebrate. They bumped heads together and said "Faith busters!" at the same time, which sounded like a bellow to Milly. Then a miracle occurred. They tried speaking in English, and triumphantly the two said, "God … did … it! God … did … it!"

Milly was so happy at the hippos' new sentence that she said, "You hippos are the best!" She loaded them into the transport van, and they were off to their new habitat, a reserved space with no fences—a sanctuary for special hippos like Gray Hippo and Little Hippo to rest in Christ for all their remaining days.

Amanda Libbers

Printed in the United States
By Bookmasters